To my dear friend Michael

Lore of the Ghost Ship

Other books by Cristina Montalva:

The Armoured Knight

Poems Published in an Anthology:

In the Circle of Eight
Pretenses
Melancholy

Lore of the
Ghost Ship

Cristina Montalva

Illustrator: Paul W Thompson

Copyright © 2011 by Cristina Montalva.

Library of Congress Control Number: 2011908465
ISBN: Hardcover   978-1-4628-7785-0
                 Softcover   978-1-4628-7784-3
                 Ebook   978-1-4628-7786-7

All rights reserved. No part of this book may be reproduced or transmitted in any form or by any means, electronic or mechanical, including photocopying, recording, or by any information storage and retrieval system, without permission in writing from the copyright owner.

This is a work of fiction. Names, characters, places and incidents either are the product of the author's imagination or are used fictitiously, and any resemblance to any actual persons, living or dead, events, or locales is entirely coincidental.

This book was printed in the United States of America.

To order additional copies of this book, contact:
Xlibris Corporation
1-888-795-4274
www.Xlibris.com
Orders@Xlibris.com
96423

Dedication

To my Canadian grandkids Nicholas and Jessica Rodriguez.

To my Chilean granddaughter Paulina Huerta.

To the three of you with Love.

Acknowledgments

I am extremely thankful to Norma Jean Gangaram, author of many children books, for her encouragement to pursue my goals.

I am grateful to Robert Thompson, my computer class teacher at the Brampton City Recreation Centre for revising the grammar in my story.

To Ricardo Meza, for providing me Chilean's folklore books.

Thanks to Paul W. Thompson, for capturing the story essence in his illustrations.

Thanks to Xlibris Corporation's team for the making of this book.

Thanks to my son Ed, my grandkids Jessica and Nicholas for being there for me in my times of computer needs.

Thanks to Alice and Christopher Saraiva for reading my story.

Thanks to Rory Humeres for his comments on this tale.

Special thanks to Raymond Dwinnell for introducing me to the Flower City Senior Centre in Brampton.

Thanks to Alicia Riquelme and Anna Inocente for their support.

Sincere thanks to all those who have supported me.

Prologue

THE FOURTEEN-YEAR-old "Chilote," was a proud native of Chiloe, the seagull's island in Chile. His island had once been part of the whole continent of South America, but centuries of crashing waves had caused the coast to crumble, creating thousands of little islands known as the Archipelago of Chiloe. The small islands are linked together by side channels.

His tiny village, scattered along the shore of the Ancud Gulf and surrounded by undulating hills, was a picturesque rural settlement in the rugged and more sheltered east coast of the Archipelago.

The young Chilote, standing at the top of the cliffs and gazing out to sea, imagined a strong vessel with huge, mighty, black sails and half-mast pitching with the waves. It radiated beams of pulsating light. The ship emerged from the ocean's depths surrounded by a thick fog.

The boy pictured the dreary lights in his mind's eye, and it was as if he could actually hear the sorrowful, chilling music on board.

He knew the stories: If a person was picked up by the vessel and found favor in the eyes of the ghosts, they would discover the boundless treasures gathered by the ship's crew from the bottom of the sea. Yet those snatched by the ship were forbidden to reveal the secret – heaven protect whoever dared to reveal it – and if they did, their days were numbered.

He was also aware that the ghost ship caught and imprisoned the souls of all those who had drowned at sea and those who encountered the vessel.

He had foreseen what happened after the ill-fated captain, demented, had cursed the sea, the weather, the ship's crew, and swore in the strongest language against God. The boy could hear the prompt answer that blasted from the heavens and saw how the waters started to bulge as foaming waves crashed over the ship. Lightning flashed, followed by thunder that rumbled like artillery. Then the gales began to howl around the ship and wailed eerily through the taut rope lines. Before long, the ship tumbled over into the raging waters.

"This is the 'Camahueto,' as we all know," Mateo had said to him. "This ghost ship terrorizes the fishermen who dare to confront it. It is said that the ship emerges from the depths of the sea in an eerie light through the fog. In the middle of raging storms, the ship's crew comes back to life with screams and wailing, because the last moment they were alive, the waters engulfed them. Their death is played out over and over again."

Chapter One

IT HAD BEEN a warmish spring day with the sun shining brightly, but it was getting chilly and dark by the time Pancho came pacing along the coarse, grey, sandy beach toward the town's few huddled "palaphitos," the humble dwellings on vertical wooden posts placed deep in the water.

These comprised, of two parts – an upper terrace, which served as a patio and a lower part, where the chilotes did their work with the boat full of fish at the edge of the water.

He put down his wicker bucket filled with mussels, clams, and crabs he had just caught in the rocky tide pools. He stopped to breathe and smelled the salty aroma of the sea and to feel the soft brush of the wind on his tanned, rosy-red cheeks. He lifted his round head covered with a trademark red bandana that tied back his long jet-black hair that fell in shaggy bangs across his forehead. He imagined he was a fisherman sailing across the seas with his boat full of nets, buckets of bait, and hoses. He shielded his eyes against the sun and peered out at the river border.

A swirling flock of frenzied seagulls shook him out of his daydream, and he watched them wade into the water as he scampered at top speed along the riverbank.

"I'm late," he said as he arrived, plodding heavily up the lane of old, humble, and unattractive dwellings that he nevertheless found appealing.

His father, Agustin, was at the baitfish eatery. He waited for him there every day, and they had preferred to dine at the Eatery especially since his mother had disappeared. She had gone out very early one morning to collect shellfish and never returned.

Pancho imagined her graceful body sliding in front of him on the rough gravel. He believed she was visiting another world and would return. But she wasn't in another world; she did not walk into the light. Her spirit was in a cave, thinking of her husband and son, only to walk out on moonlit nights, gazing from afar at the dimmed candle light in the window of her home. He hoped to find her at home, seated on the ground or at her "telar," the horizontal wooden frame fastened together with nails, weaving wool into a blanket, a poncho, a throw, or a mat. But she wasn't there. Only her fingerprints were still there. Even though the evening sun was still warm on his back, an updraft of cool air gushed over his strong, young body, sending a chill over him that made him shudder as he felt in his heart the emptiness left by his mother's absence.

Inside the baitfish eatery, the only big room with a homely fireside was swarmed with tough fishermen who swore too much. Their voices seemed shaded by echoes of "La Sirena," the most beautiful and kind mermaid with golden hair, and the ability to change her tail into human legs and whose naked body draped in seaweed was part of the islanders' mythology.

As the legend said, she was the protector of the sea creatures such as the oysters, mussels, mollusks, and shellfish. She was feared by the fishermen who believed they would be doomed to poverty if they abuse these sea creatures.

They also believed that if she danced facing the horizon, the fishing would be plentiful, but if she danced while looking at the hills, as some fishermen had seen her doing on that day, the fishing would be meager. No one dared to go fishing that day.

Pancho loved the baitfish eatery, the fishermen's meeting place, where they elbowed their way in to sit on the wooden benches. The seamen's stories fuelled his enthusiasm for the supernatural world that transported him to a place of unseen enchantment. Along with the enchantment was the ghostly tale of those uninvited out of this world being like the Camahueto, a colossal sea wolf with magical powers to wipe out nature and all living creatures, as well as to transform itself into a vessel or whatever form it wished. The source of the sea wolf powers could be pulled out by supernatural means of a machi or witch's drum. This tales intoxicated the fantasies that filled his imagination.

There, in a corner farther away Pancho's father Agustin, a very private, short, and muscular man sat at a table made from a wrecked ship's stern board. A bowl of mussel soup was already set up in front of him, but he held an empty bottle of "chicha," a fermented apple cider, in his left hand.

"I like to take a nip once in a while," he said, noticing his son's frown.

"I love this place," Pancho said, sitting down across from his father. His eyes slid toward his father's glaring eyes. "The nets and sail canvases hanging from the ceiling make me feel as if I were in a ship." Agustin nodded gloomily. "Boy, please have your mussel soup," he said, gazing sadly before him as he quietly sipped his cold soup.

After they had been eating for a while, Mateo, a clean-shaven fisherman with bright eyes and a mop of grey hair, began to walk around the tables talking to all the fishermen in the room. Pancho looked under his rolled-up pants and noticed he was wearing two pairs of stockings, one as a protection against humidity and beneath those another pair as protection against the mildew.

Mateo, a man with a sun- and wind-weathered face, was a very special fisherman. Drunk as a lord, with a huge belly, he was a likeable man with a friendly nature and who was frequently seen to be smiling. Mateo was a fast talker who would wave his hands about and gesture wildly when he spoke. His wisdom and culture he had acquired by talking and listening and by observing life. This had made him very familiar with Chiloe's jargon, and he was a treasure trove of the island's folklore, mythology, history, and superstitions. To Pancho he was a true sea dog, a sailor of many seas.

Mateo came to his brother's table, playfully punched his nephew's arm, and sat beside Agustin, facing the boy. "Things are coming to a head," the sailor said as he leaned forward and stared closely into Pancho's black eyes. "Do you wish to hear another ghost story?" he said to him. His voice was so loud the youngster felt certain his uncle could be heard a mile away.

The voices in the room suddenly ceased, complete silence arose, and no one so much as dared to breathe. The boy had a magical feeling for the supernatural story at hand, and he knew his uncle's ghostly stories had all the right ingredients for a spooky good time. Mateo told stories that made Pancho want to crawl under the floor.

"Is it about the ghost ship?" Pancho asked.

"No, it's a different one," Mateo said sarcastically.

"All I wish is to hear the ghost ship story," Pancho said, peering at the man's face. "Uncle, are you willing to tell it to me?" The rest of the fishermen holding their breath watched motionless waiting for Mateo's response.

The fisherman paused for a moment, as if to collect his thoughts. "Well, if that is what you wish, here it is."

Chapter Two

MATEO BEGAN TO whisper in a mysterious voice, arching his bushy, black left eyebrow. "It's all about the big ship called Camahueto. The name, it's believed, to be a native word from centuries ago meaning 'sea wolf.' The ship itself, as the sea wolf, has the ability to adopt different forms, like a stone, a stick, and appears and vanishes whenever it wishes. Well, now, some of the Camahueto's crew are castaways whose bodies never returned from the sea. Others are people who disappeared mysteriously.

"It so happened that one moonless night I went for a stroll to the river along a prominent path. To my surprise, I saw a beautiful, huge moon reflected on the water. I looked up but saw no moon, because no moon was in the sky. I bounded and rebounded like a loony, and I hurried to find more fishermen shouting like mad men "come to see it, come to see it, come right now!" In awe, we all burned the midnight oil watching that shapely round moon mirrored on the water. I wanted to jump into it. I was attracted to it, but I was afraid the ship would take me in and that I would be lost forever." Pancho, amazed, stared at his uncle's face. Agustin was looking cross.

"Anyway," Mateo continued, acknowledging his nephew's and brother's looks, "the ghost ship terrorizes the fishermen who dare to encounter it, as you already know."

"What happened to the ghost ship's captain?" inquired the lad, ignoring his father's eyes.

"To understand what happened to the captain, known as Domingo Mataluna, we have to go back in time, to the beginning of the whole story. The captain was madly in love with Rosita, a young town maid. They were about to get married, but he could not wait any longer to fulfill his love, so he invited the girl to the woods. She didn't want to go. It was forbidden because of The Beast's legend. The Beast who was a dwarf, malformed man, was believed to live in the woods. He was eighty centimeters in height, and his face was gruesome and hideous. His potato-like face had a wide, flat nose with nostrils which extended to the side so as to be able to smell the essence of young virgins. He wore willow's leaf clothes which hung in narrow strips from his neck to his ankles. On his squat head, he had a conical straw hat. Instead of feet, he had 'munones' like stumps of amputated limbs and carried a stone cane that helped him to walk."

Mateo heaved a sigh and, leaning against the wooden table, began filling his big clay glass of chicha from Agustin's bottle. "Well, fellows," he said, speaking slowly and winking at his audience who sat in suspense.

Pancho and every fisherman in the room watched voiceless as if waiting for permission to breathe again. Agustin groaned and turned back to his drink.

"Let's go ahead with the story. The lover pushed his intentions to go to the woods. He pleaded, declared his undying love, his passion, his desires, and the fire consuming him. The girl agreed to meet him at dusk.

"The captain was on pins and needles. At last he was going to get what he wanted. In his euphoria, he ran recklessly away from Rosita's house to celebrate with a glass of chicha. On the path to the eatery, he met an old man, his friend Don Jacinto, sitting outside the baitfish eatery. The man's eyes seemed to be looking at the horizon, as if he were expecting to see something. His faded red shirt and pants were completely wet. His face was creased with deep wrinkles. Scruffy, speckled gray hair ran along the middle of his head. The captain sat down beside the old man and told him about his forest rendezvous. The old man congratulated Domingo on his good luck and invited him to the baitfish eatery for a drink. Without noticing, time passed by.

"Meanwhile, Rosita slipped away from the house, utterly unaware of her fate. The captain suddenly became aware of the time and took off like a bat out of hell to the woods. Stumbling from the chicha stupor and barely holding himself together, he saw the girl sprinting erratically in the middle of the forest.

"He called to her, and she wailed while looking back, not stopping. He held his breath, immediately realizing that something was dreadfully wrong. He had never seen that look in her eyes. Her gentle expressive gaze had changed to something terrifying, and her bewildered eyeballs rotated in their sockets. Suddenly, her head bowed toward the ground. He took heart and, confused, dashed after her only to notice the girl's ragged clothes scattered on the grass.

"As he chased after his future bride, she let him to get within three meters and then stopped and looked at him, but this time with a look of forgiveness. He tried to talk to her, to ask what happened, but noticed the foolishness of his question. Only then he understood. "It is my fault!" he shouted, but he thought, "No, no, it wasn't my fault. She had fallen under The Beast's gaze." As the legend said, despite his repulsive looks, this being awakes in young girls an irresistible attraction and seduces them with his unique gaze. In a second, Rosita disappeared.

"When the captain reached the point where she had disappeared, he found a cliff. Looking down, he saw his bride's crushed body.

"For two months, Domingo suffered fits of despair. Rosita haunted him – wherever he went, she turned up. He admitted what he had done, but it was too late to apologize. She was dead, but she had taken possession of his soul. His feelings tormented him.

"One day he met Don Jacinto. He was the one to be blamed, the captain thought, for inviting him to the baitfish eatery. His anger boiled over, and he erupted like a volcano at the person he believed to be the cause of his misfortune.

"It wasn't your fault, his friend reassured him. The beast was the one who attacked your bride." But this revelation revolted Domingo even more. He didn't want to be around his friend anymore.

"Domingo, drawing strength out of his weakness, pushed the old man aside and rushed to his ship. After an hour or so of aimless wandering over the rubble without taking any notice, he arrived at a rural church, with a few houses around it. He looked up at the church full of surprise, and wondered, 'How did I get here?'

"It's time to go," said Agustin, standing beside his son. Pancho's father's sun-flecked hand on his shoulder snapped the boy from the story.

"Now, you all know what happened to Domingo Sarmiento and his ship," Mateo hurriedly finished.

Pancho was shocked that his father had interrupted the story, but he quickly wolfed down the rest of the cool mussel soup, wiped his mouth against the back of his left sleeve, and followed his father's lumpish walk.

Chapter Three

IT WAS COOL and dark by the time they started for home. Once more Pancho imagined his mom's graceful body gliding silently over the gravel in front of him. As they zigzagged for half a mile up the hills toward home, they passed rows of rustic cabins covered with fish hanging by the gills to dry. Both entered the dark shack's tiny room.

There was not a single photograph on the walls, not even one of Pancho's mother. A sick feeling of anguish knotted the adolescent's stomach. It was the feeling he had whenever confronted by his mother's death.

On the only table stood a half-empty glass of chicha. Agustin reached for the cider and filled the glass to the top, sat down beside the table, sighed, and slowly sipped his drink.

"It's a way to relax," he said apologetically. For some minutes, he did not speak.

Pancho, for his part, did not feel he could start to talk, but his eyes glanced across at his father's blank eyes.

He felt bitter and wished his father would stop drinking and start looking after the smacks in the floating dock which were waiting for repairs. For a month, he had been neglecting his work. He missed being around his father when working. He was lonely, and he was beginning to feel more and more disconnected from his father day by day.

"Father, will you stay with me tonight? Since mother disappeared, you go out every night," he said abruptly.

"No, sonny. I'll be in my boat for a while," Agustin said. "It needs to be caulked, and I've already mixed the algae, clay, and fish fat." He sat and sunk his head upon his chest.

He had built the boat, and although it was frail, Pancho was proud of his father's skills at repairing and building canoes for the town's fishermen.

Pancho's eyes bulged as he tried to restrain his tears, and he dabbed them away with the back of his hands, but he got up the nerve to ask, "Why do you really go there?"

After a dreadful silence, Agustin stared at his son with deep sorrow. "Really, I go there looking for your mom," he said sighing, closed his eyes as if he were searching for her in the blackness of his drunkenness. "Do you miss her?"

"Yes, a lot. Sometimes I think she is on the ghost ship," Pancho replied.

"Your mother isn't there, Pancho. Her spirit is not on the ghost ship, like the ones who perished at sea, but in heaven. She had the gentleness of the moon and deserves heaven for all her good thoughts and deeds. Yes, she is in heaven, and we must believe so, but there are things that happen that we can't explain."

The boy stood still beside his father in the shadowy room. He sobbed with heartache. Nothing had been the same after her death. And yet it was the truth to him that many people who died at sea ended up on the Camahueto. "I want to go with you!"

"Sorry, son, you must go to sleep," Agustin said closing the door behind him.

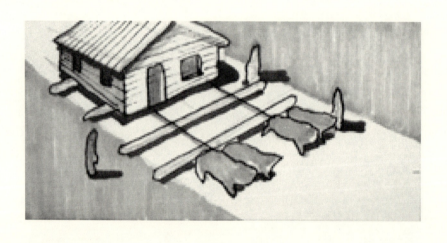

Chapter Four

DRAINED, PANCHO SNUGGLED under his woven throw and fell into a slumber.

He dreamed of the ghost ship in the waves and the fog, the ghost ship's captain prowling and dragging his father out of his barge, his mother's eyes gleaming, and her lovely body gliding in the open air. She was enveloped in a brilliant blaze of light, and a stream of iridescent energy radiated from around her, as she reached out for his father's hand.

Next morning, Agustin and Pancho woke up with the sunrays streaming through a cluster of clouds. The terrors of the dream subsided with the awakening light of the new day, and yet he was surprised that the images of his dreadful dream were still in the forefront of his mind. He was eager to share his dream with his father. It was easy for him to talk to his father after the chicha stupor had faded from his head.

"You had your dream because my brother's story blew your mind away shortly before your bedtime. Anyhow, it's also because you're holding your mom's memory in your heart," Agustin responded after his son vividly described the dream.

Pancho was relieved that his dream was in the open, and he experienced new strength as he stood outside on the peak of the small hill where his shack stood.

Below him, the larch and myrtle trees were pinched here and there in the sparkling light of the morning dew. Further on, a flock of seagulls flew across the beautiful blue sky, and the gentle breeze of the hills filled him with joy.

"C'mon, boy!" Agustin shouted from down the path. "It's time for us to go to the Minga." He hastened down the pebbled pathway while Pancho dashed behind him, glancing at the ramp on the beach where friends and neighbors were arriving one by one or in couples to take part in the Minga.

Chapter Five

"YES, IT'S THE Minga day. We haven't had a Minga for a long time!" he exclaimed, his heart beating with enthusiasm.

Pancho knew that a Minga was the oldest of Chiloe's living traditions. It reflected the islanders' good disposition and willingness to help each other whenever labor was needed. Although this was his first Minga, he knew that Mingas were for all kinds of agricultural tasks such as plowing fields, reaping potatoes, cutting wood, chopping and trimming trees, and even repairing the roofs of houses and helping newlyweds to settle. What's more, the "mingueros" did not receive payment for their work. Their recompense was a splendid and plentiful meal and wine prepared by those that the Minga was for.

"You're right, Pancho. We're gathering to help Pedro move his house to another location on the island across the channel."

"Why is he moving?"

"Because he's scared that the ghost of the previous owner inhabits the surroundings of the house."

"But Pedro has adorned the larch trees with the hoses and hooks that the ghost most liked when he was alive," queried Pancho.

"Although he adorned the trees, he does not dare to live on this island any longer." Agustin pretended to be gruff to put an end to his son's questions.

"Father, do you know how far the house is to be carried?"

"The distance is about three kilometers, and it's a grueling, day-long process. We'll be working from sunup to sundown. We must hurry. Since we overslept, the work must be already halfway done."

It didn't take long to arrive at the grounds, where the mingueros had already cut the larch trees into smooth, round rollers.

"Yeah! Here are Agustin and Pancho!" some mingueros yelled at the top of their lungs. Although it was almost midday, they didn't mention how late they were. Nodding and smiling, the villager in charge shouted, "Over here!"

"Pancho, you're to help the men get the stalks and tie them together with the strong straw ropes to prepare the wagon where the house is to be placed," the leader said.

"Ha, ho!" laughed the boy. "I can do that for sure!" he said, running to where the wood piles were. "I'll work hand in hand with my friends."

Meanwhile, the organizer, Agustin and other villagers were yoking six huge, white and black oxen together to move the house.

It was mid-afternoon when the "birloche," or wagonet, which is a kind of open sleigh, was ready to be connected to the yoke of the animals by means of a metal chain.

"You've done a perfect job in placing the rollers two meters from each other," the overseer said, looking at each man and placing his hand on Pancho's shoulder. It was the time to move the house from the wooden structures.

"This house doesn't have a base!" Pancho exclaimed, amazed to see the empty place where the house had stood moments before.

"This is because," said his uncle standing beside him, "all the houses on the island are raised on wooden supports to prevent the devastating humidity that filters through the floor."

After the house was placed on the birloche and carried with the help of the oxen, they arrived at the cove where it was placed on the water and tied to a yellow motorboat, ready to be dragged to the other islet.

"Dad, the house's roof looks like a colorful turtle shell," Pancho blurted, studying the scene. "I really want to watch it until it gets to the other side."

"Well, all in all, it really is a sight to watch the house floating across the river," his father conceded.

The day had worn down. The sun was low, and the sky was becoming darker as they hurried to where the house was already placed on its horizontal support of wooden boards.

"At last, evening has come! Let's go to the good night food circle," Pancho said, smelling the aroma of the food. The good night food circle was the half-meter wide underground smoke oven, made out of a hole dug in the ground with large stones and a fire inside.

"The fire is good, and the stones are hot, and I can see the shellfish, the clams, and the mussels. The layers of meat, smoked sausages, potatoes, and vegetables are a feast to my eyes, and the smell of the food is driving me crazy!" Pancho said, while filling his clay plate with shellfish, vegetables, two small smoked sausages, and his favorite "milcao," a potato bread cooked at the top of the high flame.

"Mmmm! The shellfish have released their water. Delicious."

"Yes, son. When the steam rises from the shell, it shows that all is flavored and the layers above are cooked, are ready to eat." His senses were also treated with the sight and the smells of the "curanto," the typical dish of Chiloe.

"They have lit more campfires than on any other night before!" he exclaimed while eating. Soon afterward, they all gathered around the crackling fires and sat on the grass, where Mateo was already entertaining youngsters with simple charades, which adults and kids were trying to guess.

"Come, Pancho!" hurried his uncle. "I have a riddle for you. I'll give you three clues."

"Hanging ruddy. Furry, staring. What is it?"

"The meat and the cat!" Pancho guessed, correctly. It wasn't long, though, until he was chewing and swallowing his food again. All the mingueros were becoming high spirited and cheerful with the rounds of chicha, and in no time, they were magnificently stuffed with the food.

They ate and drank to their heart's content.

Chapter Six

AT DUSK, THE bonfire's light sparkled like stars in the ebony of the night. The boy looked at the animals, the people, and beyond these, the open countryside out under the darkened sky.

The air was cooling, and the moonlight shimmered on the river with little silver sparkles of light.

"I must be patient and wait for the right moment to find out the end of the ghost ship story," he muttered to himself.

Mateo was still amusing the islanders with his humorous brainteasers, and little by little everyone started to grow sluggish and quiet. It was the opportunity his nephew had been waiting for.

"Uncle, tell us the end of the captain's story," he pleaded, sitting quietly beside his uncle. For a moment, the forest was silent . . .

"Well," Mateo answered, cocking one eyebrow and staring at his nephew for a second, before cracking a grin.

Finally, all the youngster had to do was wrap up in his poncho, lean backward over the spruce branches and moose leaves, and let his ears pave the highway of his imagination back to the magic of the captain's underworld.

The storyteller settled down, nodded, leaned closer, and began. It felt as if his tale had hardly been interrupted.

"Now then, where were we? We left Domingo in front of the town church. 'How did I get here?' Domingo said, full of surprise. Only then he noticed a few houses nestled around the church. He looked up at the wooden church made of silver larch and cypress trees, with green wooden shingles and the weathered and aged belfry. He knew that the bell tower was the only piece of the original building that remained from the old construction by the Jesuits during the eighteenth to nineteenth centuries."

"Who were the Jesuits, Uncle?" Pancho interrupted.

"They were members of the Roman Catholic religious order from Spain, who settled down in our archipelago and took advantage of the island's abundant and excellent timber. And as you know, even the original wooden pegs have been replaced by nails. This was because of the termites and humidity which forced us to replace parts over the years. Now back to the captain.

"A stroke of the bell churned his emotions up, and at the borderline of his insanity, he saw the church as a salvation to liberate him from his bondage. While he staggered back and forth, he lurched through the open church door and into the central nave, and he heard a man singing. The voice echoed around him, shaking him with grief. He swayed as he stood for a minute holding his breath.

"Domingo hesitated for a moment as if awakening from a trance. The priest's voice sent him further into turmoil. Standing beside the basin of holy water, he punched it, splashing it all over the floor.

"'Stop right there. Sacrilege. My god!' the priest, dumbstruck shouted. He paused, and then marched in fury toward the intruder who knocked an old statue of Saint John to the ground as if a demon were controlling his arm. The statue hit the priest who slipped on the water and hit his head on a pew. There was a dull thud, accompanied by a crack. The priest cried out in pain and stifled a gasp.

"The captain's heart pounded as he knelt beside the prostrated body. Touching the priest's forehead, it felt cold under his hand. The thought of the dead churchman made him shudder, and, as if awakening from his madness, he screamed: 'Oh god, what I have done!'"

"In a state of deepest misery and resentment, a groan burst from his throat, and wheeling to the flowery altar, his eyes scanned the aisles only then noticing that the church was adorned with garlands of bright white roses and white copihues, the national flower of Chile. The benches were dressed with spruce leaves for the celebration of the Jesus of Nazareth festivities.

"He went insane literally and turned purple in anger. An explosion of rage erupted behind his eyes, and stammering, he charged like a mad bull, lashing out with fury and pain and knocking the candle stand, the flowers, the altar cloth, and the Bible to the floor.

"He staggered behind the altar shrine, and opened the wafer box. The paten bowl was already filled with the communion Hosts. He hurled them, and the wafers landed right and left on the floor. He trampled on them, stopping only when they were impregnated with the bloodstained roses' color.

"Domingo came back to the niches and saw the monstrance wherein the consecrated Host was exposed for veneration. It was a small, gold-plated receptacle two or three inches in diameter with a crafted silver cross at the top. In the middle was set a glass case that had belonged to the church from the time of its construction more than one hundred years ago. It was the town's pride!

"The captain seized the piece with the intention of breaking it, but at that moment, a group of curious neighbors, alarmed by the loud noise, entered. One look at the church was enough for them to realize what had taken place in there.

"'Good heavens, Domingo! What have you done?' one shouted.

"'Are you not God-fearing?' his friend Jacinto asserted. He had showed up and was curious to find out what the cause of the turmoil was.

"'What God?' The captain replied. 'How can you say that God exists if my life is doomed? What a rotten life! You and your beliefs are not real.'

"Suddenly, for a minute or two, the captain became quiet, motionless, and as he awoke from his madness, his body trembled. 'What have I done?' he screamed. He took a step back, turned around, then fuming, reacted.

Carrying the receptacle of the Holy Host, he ran toward the exit.

"'For heaven's sake, leave the Host!' somebody shouted, but Domingo turned a deaf ear. In great haste, he pushed his way through the crowd and took off, followed by the revolted neighbors. Impelled by his insanity and still carrying the monstrance, he managed at breakneck speed to escape to his ship, with Jacinto following in the footsteps of his captain."

Chapter Seven

"AT THE CRACK of dawn Domingo and Jacinto arrived at the Camahueto, its sails nudged by the wind. Some fishing boats were propped in the quay.

"On the deck, the captain wavered around in circles, getting nowhere. The crew was taken by surprise to see their confident and determined skipper in such a pitiful state, muttering and toppling over. Worse still though, they were in shock when he flung the monstrance between bundles of ropes. Hushed silence fell over the seamen.

"'The captain is a Jonah, the one who will bring us bad luck,' one of the seafaring men whispered.

"'What are you saying?' barked Jacinto. 'Go back to your toil. Heave up the anchor! At full blast!'

"'Aye, aye skipper,' the men shouted. The ship put out to sea. A gentle breeze coming from the west pushed the vessel from behind. The first hours under sail were frenzied, with everyone double-checking their tasks. The sea was calm for several hours. Some sea dogs argued over bunk space in the seamen's cabin.

"By then the Camahueto was running with the wind, the helmsman at the wheel, a sailor in the bosun's chair at the top of the mast. Jacinto, the chief mate, took charge of navigation, but the vessel needed its captain. The crew were sullen, resentful of being forsaken by their captain.

"There was no spirit of cooperation among them and no respect for their skipper. Jacinto was well aware that chances were that the crew would not do their best.

"It was night, and a full moon lit up the sea. The head-master patrolled the deck while the watch time was taken up with trimming sails. The Camahueto was keeping a steady course. On deck, some men sat on barrels drinking and playing cards. Out of the blue, they watched the withered captain's figure sheathed in a loose black robe emerge from his cabin. He swayed as he stood in front of them. The sailors were surprised, since he was nowhere to be seen since they had left the cove. No one dared to meet his glare.

"Then the captain howled in a cavernous, abysmal, powerful voice unlike any ever uttered by humankind: 'This is my pride's punishment for my blasphemy, my scorn, and my contempt for my sins against God, my church, and my people. The time to pay is near!'

"The crew was filled with terror. A menacing blanket of fear came over them. They believed the captain might infuriate God who would send a storm onto them.

"'You will have a choice,' continued the captain. 'Those ones who stay with me on the Camahueto will live eternally, but they will lose their souls. Those who decide to jump into the waters will find death, and their souls will be saved, except for one, who will survive to tell of the events that are about to take place on my ship.'

"Now, the crew sensed they were really at death's door and were afraid for their own lives. A terror-stricken trance descended on them.

"'From this day on, the Camahueto will gather all those souls cast away and those whose fear has made them lose their grip on sanity,' ended the captain.

"Without warning, massive clouds gathered above the ship and within seconds turned black. Thunder rumbled through the heavens, and a howling wind whipped over the ship like a jerking hand intent on lashing them. The sails flapped, the waves, now more than three meters high, surged as though a gigantic claw was lifting the vessel out of the water.

"'Reef the sails!' someone shouted, but doing so was out of the question. No one dragged or tied them down.

"'Batten the hatches!' someone else screamed. No one heard the command to secure covers over the open hatches, and water kept flowing in.

"Some sailors dashed out from the forecastle, the crew's quarters, and scurried up the stairs to the main deck. Others, confused, lost control, and in complete disarray, scrambled from stern to bow, then from starboard to port. Feverish agitation grew as their cries escalated. The air was filled with horrific noise – sailors' shouts, clanking chains, and the shrills of the lines and wires which flew in chaos above their heads.

"The boom broke in half, spilling massive blocks everywhere, which fell on some of the men and killed them. No hand was at the wheel.

"The captain – in his cabin mocking and insulting God – his crew, and his ship, stood with open arms awaiting his fate. The ship was flung back and forth, pirouetting with every wave.

"Other sailors who had been running on the deck tried to jump overboard, but they were restrained by their fears and instead chose to hide in their quarters below their blankets, trying in vain to survive. A few seamen, without thinking, took one look at the gloomy sky and threw themselves into the turbulent waters, thereby saving their souls.

"The ship had been ripped in half like a sheet of paper; the only sound was that of the clapping water engulfing the ship and then . . . complete silence."

Chapter Eight

"BUT, UNCLE, THE captain had said that one of the crew was to be saved," interrupted Pancho.

"You are right. What comes next is very important to you, boy," replied Mateo. "It will stun you more than the captain's story, and it will put you in awe of Juanito, one of your ancestors."

"At the time, Juanito was fifteen years old. He stood five feet tall, and his body was like a strong, slender, larch tree. Everyone said he was the most wide awake hand on board. Although he had only joined the ship a year earlier, and without former experience, he learned to take charge of the ship's duties as cabin boy, doing errands such as running messages for the captain, helping as the kitchen boy, washing dishes and pots, and waiting on tables for the captain and crew. Moreover, he took care of the sails, ropes, and lines in all kinds of weather, and sometimes, in good weather, was even allowed to hold the wheel to keep it on course. To sum up, he was a jack of all trades.

"At the time the stormy sea began to batter the ship, Juanito was sleeping on his bunk. He woke up to a strange bump and, startled, leaned over to look down. What he saw chilled his heart like ice. Water covered the floor. He jumped out of his bed, and stumbling up and down, made his way upstairs to the deck.

"It didn't take long for him to realize they were sinking, and then he remembered the captain's bloodcurdling words: 'Only one of the crew will survive.' He made up his mind to jump into the sea. He was within one inch of falling from the rail when a fragment of the flag got stuck in his pants, holding him back. He tried to break loose, but it was no use. 'Help me, I can't jump,' he shouted, but the berserk wretched sea dogs, could neither hear nor help him.

"After a few tries, he snapped himself free. He was loose. Not knowing what force drove him, he rushed to the captain's cabin. What he saw there terrified him more than the storm. The captain's eyes were flashing and looked like they were about to jump out of their sockets.

"'Butt out,' the captain growled, aiming a vicious kick at Juanito, who wiggling, crouched down between the captain's arms and legs and saw the monstrance floating on the water. He stretched forward and took hold of it. Sneaking past his captain, he ran to the deck and climbed the boarding edge. He hesitated for a few seconds, held his breath, grasped the monstrance with all his might, and jumped overboard into the murky water.

"'Woe is me. I'm going to die,' he blubbered, trembling and quivering. He had given up, but a voice in his heart encouraged him: 'No, I will not die. I refuse to.' Jerking his arms, he managed to heave his head to the surface of the water, but the water was pulling him down."

"What happened to my forefather and the monstrance?" Pancho inquired.

"Hold it, son. You're ahead of the story," Agustin responded, sipping his chicha.

"Here is what happened," added the man. "Well, Juanito woke up. 'Where am I?' he mumbled, although dazed.

"'Be still,' a soothing voice responded. 'You are safe at home.'

"'You don't know . . . You don't understand . . .' he woozily mumbled. Only then did he grasp that he was alive and that he was tightly holding the monstrance. With everything that had happened on the ship coming back to him, Juanito wept, both with joy for being alive and with sorrow for the loss of his crewmates. He realized how lucky he was to have survived the horrendous tragedy. Then, overwhelmed, he fainted.

"The following day, Martita, his grandmother, brought him a large bowl with a light, warm chicken broth. She intended to take the monstrance from Juanito's arms.

"'No, no. I can't be separated from it,' he shouted, shaking his head from side to side.

"'Quiet down. The monstrance will be near to your pillow. Have your soup. You have not eaten for a week since we found you lying on the beach at the point of your last breath,' Martita said, feeding him the soup. 'You were feverish, and we were afraid for your life, so we called the machi, the town healer, who by means of her herbs and potions, was finally able to heal you.'

"As soon as he was left alone, Juanito looked around the room closely. His gaze stopped at the window. The ocean! The fears and anguish of his dreadful experience were revived. He sank down in terror, screaming so loudly his grandma hastened to his room.

"'I never again want to live in this palaphito, and I never again wish to look at the sea!'

"'My boy, take heart! I'll make arrangements with the priest, but for now just sleep.'

"At a very early hour on the following morning, Martita gathered the townsfolk in the church. She told them of Juanito's fears of the ocean, and they decided that the best place for him to live was in the valley, behind the little hill that served as the church's wall.

"Once the boy had settled down in his new place he looked through the window, and the church's belfry caught his eye. With that sight, he leaned back on his bed and falling soundly asleep, stayed in bed for two days.

"In the years thereafter, Juanito would give the monstrance to the town priest at every church celebration or festivity, and the priest at the end of the procession would hand it back to him.

"In addition, he gave to the townsfolk a detailed account of what had taken place on the ghost ship, of its ill-fated captain, crew, and of himself, the living proof of the captain's words: 'One of the crew will be saved, and he will be the one to tell of the events on the Camahueto.' This story has been told and retold from generation to generation across time, and so will be, for future generations to come."

Chapter Nine

A RADIANT ORANGE, yellow, and white glow in the eastern sky signaled the approach of dawn. One after the other, the mingueros roused from their slumber, grabbed their knitted ponchos and blankets, and they took off to do their daily toils.

Pancho and his father lingered in Pedro's new place for the rest of the morning. Afterward, they sat for hours on Agustin's boat, facing the horizon. They had a silent agreement to be at that moment in the place where Pancho's mother had disappeared. At sundown, it was time to return to their empty home. They were exhausted and drained.

That night Pancho climbed into his bed and curled under the blankets. Tears stung his eyes, and he turned away from his father who was slurping chicha as if it were water.

"Father, I know you really go out there, staying in the shadows all night, and although you look for mother and the ghost ship, you never find them." Agustin sat on the side of his son's bed and stroked his head.

"I know, but it doesn't matter, son. After mother died, I made myself a promise not to ever talk to you about the ghost ship. But before I leave, I'll light a candle, and hope she'll see it and be guided home. Good night, son. I'll be in the boat all night," he said, and headed for the door.

"Nothing had been the same since mother's death," Pancho thought before his mind stilled for the night, with the moon glinting at him through the window.

Pancho woke up startled, rolled over, and rubbed the sleep out of his eyes. His father's howl still echoed in his ears. He sat up to find Mateo, shirtless, standing in front of him in the pitch dark. Pancho waited motionless.

"We've found your father's empty barge propped up on the barrier reef," Mateo said. The youngster jumped out of bed and hurriedly got dressed.

"Where is he?"

"Everyone is wondering. Your father is nowhere to be found."

"What do you mean? You've got to go look for him on the seas!" Pancho bit his lower lip to keep from sobbing.

"Nay, he's dead," Mateo said.

"Maybe to you and someone else he's dead, but I know he's on the ghost ship," Pancho spluttered. "You must bring him back."

The youngster ran down to the coast and stood looking at the horizon, hoping that he might see the ghost ship. Mopping sweat from his brows, he crept back to his shed to prepare a plan and rest. His quest was risky, but he was determined to rescue his father and would be on the lookout for a boat. In the harbor, there were other fishermen searching for his father's body.

At low tide, he dashed barefooted down a steep path to the rocky tide pools to fetch "cochayuyo," a shellfish algae to soothe the starving crocodiles that panged in his belly.

Suddenly, a huge wave toppled walls of water over him. It slithered down on his body, tearing at his bedraggled clothes. The wind blasted through his soaked shirt and dripping hair. Pancho tried to hold onto a rock to steady his balance, but the rogue wave swept him right off his feet; he tumbled down the slippery rocks into the turbulent waters. A whirlpool of water sucked him down. He swung, trying to pull himself over the waves, only to be overcome by the next one. He was gripped with fear as he was wheeled about, twirling and twisting in frantic strokes, coughing water and gasping for air. His last memory before he blacked out was the sight of his father standing on the ghost ship's deck. Fog swirled around him.

Chapter Ten

WHEN HE AWOKE, woozy and limp, his father was pulling him up onto a ship. Soon, he was heaved on board the ship's deck. There were shouts and lots of bustling going on around him. Dazed, he spouted seawater, his whole body shuddering with the effort.

"You're alive!" exclaimed Agustin, bending toward his son. Spellbound, Pancho glanced at his father, but soon his happiness changed to terror. His father's eyes had a ghastly look. Agustin's hair was hoary. His once fit and muscular body had changed to a scraggy spectral brilliance!

The boy's teeth chattered as he saw the wild-eyed captain in a black cape lashed to the ship's wheel. "Father, you and the captain are dead!" Standing and trembling, he made the sign of a cross over him. "I'm lost. I'll be part of these walking dead," he muttered shivering. He knew no one ever lived after the sight of the ghost ship.

"I knew you would come," his father said, his voice deep in sorrow, then handed a faded poncho to his son.

"I can save you if you come ashore with me," Pancho said, grasping his father's arm.

"Because the ship is trapped in the ghostly underworld, I cannot leave. This is also my fate, but you're the only one who can put an end to the misery of the ghost ship's crew."

"Dad, you can leave! I must tell you about a dream I had, where mother was reaching out her hand to guide you to the light."

Agustin looked at his son in awe. "Maybe there is something you can do."

"How could I help?"

"Gather the families who believe they've lost kinsmen on the seas. You'll perform a ritual, a ceremony like our forefathers did to chase away evil spirits."

"I don't know anything about that."

"When the time comes, you'll know what to do," Agustin said, looking at the mast's sails.

The gale waned, and an eerie silence came over the sea. The busy crew stood still. The captain was no longer at the wheel. "My shipmates have fallen into a trance. Now is the time for you to leave," he said and quickly broke free a weathered boat attached to the ship's side. "Hurry up!" he shouted. "Get into the dinghy."

As the boat slithered down the ropes, Pancho stood staring up at his fathers' phantasmagorical face. With a flop and a wobble, the boat fell into the water. The ghost ship and its ghostly cargo vanished so quickly that the lad couldn't track when it happened. Dumbfounded, he peered out at the empty space.

"I'll be adrift in the ocean!" he mumbled to himself, "I'm lost." His stomach fluttered. "No, I can't be scared. I have a task at hand." So, following his thought, he wildly paddled back to shore, allowing the current and the wind to help him.

By the time he pulled up on the beach, he was exhausted. He lay there stunned, his eyes half closed as ruddy-faced fishermen swarmed around him. Mateo carried him up to the baitfish eatery where freshly made steamed muzzle soup was served to the youngster by a young woman. After the soup, Pancho felt sleepy. "Although you want to know what happened to me, you'll have to wait," he murmured as his head bobbled.

"Maybe later he will tell us more," Mateo agreed. "Let him rest."

Chapter Eleven

NEXT MORNING, THE boy woke up on a bed at the baitfish eatery. Later, in between sips of milky tea, he told of his encounter with his father on the ghost ship.

"The way to help him and his shipmates escape their eternal fate is to make them clothes from netting, the meshed strands interweaved that we use to catch fish. The netted clothes will catch and hold everything evil. The pure in heart will pass through the webbing and will find the way to freedom."

"I can bring your father's silver coins from his wooden chest," prompted Mateo. "With them we can lure the greedy spirits."

Pancho approved and continued, "First, this has to be done only by the next of kin of those lost at seas," he said, taking another sip. "Secondly, we are to go to the beach where the cinnamon, the sacred tree, stands. We'll place abundant food and the silver offerings there along with the netted clothes. Also, I will tie my ring onto my father's net." Pancho stopped for a second to see if people agreed with him and saw everyone's nod.

"Next, we'll make the 'cultrum,' a circular wooden receptacle twenty centimeters in diameter, which will serve as a drum. Inside it, we'll place small, never used quartz stones, as well as silver coins, healing herbs, and birds' feathers. Finally, no one can touch the ghosts. Otherwise, the purpose of the ceremony will be lost forever." He wondered how he had come up with all these ideas. "Well," he said, "that is all."

Months went by as the preparations for the ceremony were made. Three days before the night of San Juan, the winter solstice on June 21, they hung the knitted nets on the sacred tree. Pancho, the crew's next of kin, painted their bodies in white and red plant pigments, and around their torsos, they wore chains made of silver conical coins and conical rows of silver bells linked together. The women wore them around their foreheads and on their colorful dresses.

For three days, they chanted and danced to the beat of drums. The dance consisted of three quick steps in place, one beat per step, and on the fourth beat, there was a rising of the knee. Then the pattern repeats, starting with the opposite foot. They blew horns and little whistles cast in silver. The silver ornaments jingled in a tinkling sound to chase away malevolent spirits. The machi danced around the sacred tree, playing the cultrum, which, played by her, became a magical drum.

On the third night of the ceremony, lightning exploded over their heads. There was a moment when Pancho looked up and gazed at the horizon. There, gleaming like a dark island in the watery depth, the ghost ship loomed.

Suddenly, a vast contingent of spirits floated down from the ship. Barely visible in the gloom of the darkened sky and the dark blue sea, they glided above the water toward the beach. It was an eerie sight. "Is this is a chimera, a product of my imagination, a trick on my eyes, or a fantasy created by me? No, all is real. It's happening right in front of me!" Pancho was in awe, and his heart sped up and skipped a beat with the expectation of seeing his father again. As he looked out, Agustin came forth carrying on his back a weathered bag with a wooden chest in it. Then the ship's spirits, eager to regain their souls, tried on one knitted net after another. When they did not pass through them, they threw them down around the sacred tree.

At that moment, as the full moon sat over the cinnamon tree, Pancho's mother appeared, her celestial body to be seen only by her son and the machi, while the islanders continued dancing and chanting, not aware of what was happening around them.

After that, all changed to a dream state, a slow and peaceful motion for Pancho. To him, his mother's body sparkled in by the light of the moon and was covered by a transparent silver cloudlike veil. Her brown hair was adorned by shining stars. Her presence brought peace to the ghosts, who slowly slipped into the knitted nets. In doing so, they became visible to human eyes. No longer were they enslaved.

Meanwhile, Agustin found the net with the ring; however, before he tried it on, he placed the old bag on the sand. As soon as he slipped the net over his head, he became visible to all, and at this instant, he saw his wife by his side. They embraced while their son hurried to join them; his head pillowed between father and mother. The moonlight enveloped them as they remained clinched to one another. After a while Agustin handed the chest to his child.

"Son, this is my present to you for your strength, bravery, and love for others. You took the challenge and completed the task."

Pancho took it without opening it and placed it on the sand. Just then the captain joined them and hugged the youngster.

"We are no longer prisoners in the ghost ship. You have opened the gate to heaven where freedom is," he said. "You will be part of the legend for generations to come, and the ghost ship will be an empty vessel as a reminder of it." With a kind smile, he sauntered to where his crew stood.

Pancho was euphoric – at last he was with his parents. "I know this will last only for now. It is like a dayfly that will last for today, and I am thankful for it," he said to his parents.

"You are right, son," his mother said, gently touching her son's forehead and smiling. "Our souls will soon leave the physical self, as the physical self no longer served us. So our bodies will return to the Earth and will become dust. I know that your father and I might not be here for you in body, but we will be always in your heart, and you can also sense us in every rock, in flower, even in the wind."

Pancho noticed that life was slowly fading from her voice. At the same time, a white ray of moonlight moved swiftly toward them, and while her silky words still echoed in his ears, Pancho gazed at his parents until they melted into the light that receded to the sky, followed by the other spirits fading into the thin air. They had gone to the great beyond.

Afterward, the souls whose nets did not fit returned back to the Camahueto. That's why the ghost ship will continue to navigate the Archipelago of Chiloe for years to come.

References

ALTHOUGH THE CHARACTERS and plot in this book are of my own invention, I am indebted to the work of the following authors who have provided great insight into the culture, folklore and environment of the location in which the story is set.

Emmerich, Fernando. Leyendas chilenas. Chile: Editorial Andres Bello. Plc., 1994

Haverbeck, Erwin. Relatos orales de Chiloe. Chile: Editorial Andres Bello. Plc., 1989

Lagos, Ovidio. Chiloe. Un Mundo Separado. Argentina: Editorial El Ateneo. Plc., 2006

Perez, Floridor. Mitos y leyendas de Chile. Santiago de Chile: Editorial Zig-Zag, S.A. 1992

Internet. Chiloe's web sites

Author's Biography

CRISTINA MONTALVA WAS born in Santiago, Chile to a middle class family and was educated in Liceo de Ninas # 1 Javiera Carrera. While working as a teacher, she studied psychology at the Universidad Catolica in Santiago.

Montalva as a young girl living in Chile, desired of becoming a full time writer, but main events such as marriage, raising a family, immigrating to Canada, graduating with a HARP certificate at George Brown college, working as a dental assistant and carving out a career at the Transformational Arts College in Toronto as Spiritual Psychotherapist left little time to write.

Cristina Montalva wrote the first draft of LORE of the GHOST SHIP in 2001 for a course through the Institute of Children Literature. Although Montalva is not a native of the Chiloe's Archipelago, the inspiration for this story came out of her Chilean background from a folktale her grandmother used to tell her. This tale remained in her head for decades.

Montalva, wrote the longer version of LORE of the GHOST SHIP with only a memory at first, later on looked at some notes she took while vacationing in Chile from an interview and books readings and Internet sites, who gave her vital information on the legends and customs of Chiloe.

Cristina Montalva is a member of the Brampton Arts Council and has also volunteered for the All Star Reading Program at St. Cecilia Elementary School in Brampton, as well as a client support volunteer for the Dorothy Ley Hospice in Etobicoke.

The highlight of Cristina Montalva's writing life was receiving the 2006 Arts Acclaim Award for her first children's picture book "The Armoured Knight."

Montalva lives in Brampton. She is close to her grandkids which allows her to be very active in their lives. She is also close to Nicholas' friends: Brandon, Erica, Ian and Nicole.

Edwards Brothers, Inc.
Thorofare, NJ USA
August 11, 2011